SPLASHING
BY THE Shore

Beach Activities for Kids

LisA MullArkey

Illustrations by
Debra Spina Dixon

Gibbs Smith, Publisher

TO ENRICH AND INSPIRE HUMANKIND

Salt Lake City | Charleston | Santa Fe | Santa Barbara

To my mom and dad for putting the sand between my toes and the wind in my sails. — LM

I dedicate this book to my kids, Ellery and Jack. — DD

First Edition
11 10 09 08 07   5 4 3 2 1

Published by
Gibbs Smith, Publisher
P.O. Box 667
Layton, Utah 84041

Orders: 1.800.748.5439
www.gibbs-smith.com

Designed by Dawn DeVries Sokol
Printed and bound in Hong Kong

Library of Congress Cataloging-in-Publication Data
Mullarkey, Lisa.
   Splashing by the shore : beach activities for kids / Lisa Mullarkey;
   illustrations by Debra Spina Dixon.—1st ed.
      p. cm.
   ISBN-13: 978-1-58685-884-1
   1. Beaches—Recreational use—Juvenile literature. 2. Outdoor
recreation—Juvenile literature. 3. Outdoor games—Juvenile literature.
   I. Title.
GV191.62.M85 2007
796.5'3—dc22
                        2006020326

Contents

Introduction

Put on your sunglasses, slather on sunscreen, and head to the beach to catch a wave! What could be better than the sand, sun, and surf? Whether you live by the beach, rent a lake house for the summer, or spend a week vacationing seaside, you can't beat digging your toes into the shimmering sand and splashing by the shore.

I grew up near the beach and played there all summer! With miles of sand and surf to explore, there was never a dull moment. I became a beach bum . . . and an expert! I spent hours strolling along the shore, adding to my shell collection, flying kites with friends, building sand castles, boogie boarding, and playing endless hours of volleyball and horseshoes.

With this book, you can feel like an expert, too. You'll uncover the mysteries of tide pools, make sand-sational crafts, and play some fun games in and out of the water. When you can't get to the real beach, you can throw a beach party. This book gives you great ideas and fun activities to bring the beach to you any time of the year!

Get Ready
for the Beach!

Most people throw on a bathing suit, drape a towel around their neck, and head right to the beach. But to make sure you have a fun-filled day at the beach, you need to know what to bring and how to stay safe.

Do not leave home without...

- Beach towels

- Waterproof sunscreen, lip balm with sunscreen, and sunglasses

- Sandals, a wide-brimmed hat, and a cover-up for when you've had enough sun

- Cooler with water, snacks, and ice

- Large beach bag to cart items to the beach

- Buckets, shovels, and sand castle molds

- Beach ball, rafts, and boogie boards

- Beach umbrella (sometimes you can rent one)

- Beach badges (call ahead to find out if your beach requires them; pin them to someone's beach chair so you won't forget them or have to search through your beach bag to find them)

BEACH ETIQUETTE

When you're sharing the biggest playground in the world with hundreds of other people, it's important to be polite and thoughtful. To help keep everyone's tempers cool in the blazing sun, follow these easy rules.

1. Before you set everything up, look around. Choose an area that isn't too close to another group.

2. Don't feed the seagulls. Who wants a flock of birds swooping overhead for sandwich pieces and leaving—umm—a little mess behind?

3. Make trash? Take trash! When you leave the beach, don't leave your garbage behind. Look for a trash can or take it with you.

4. Shake sand out of your towel by gathering its four corners. Walk to an area where there aren't any people and shake the sand from your towel gently.

5. Don't knock down any sculptures or sand castles that aren't your own.

6. Running in loose sand will make it blow and fall onto people. Save your running for the water's edge!

7. Leave glass containers at home. Broken glass is dangerous to bare feet. Ouch!

8. If you have a radio, be respectful of your neighbors. A blaring radio isn't beach-friendly.

Most towns post rules for their beach. Some rules might be: No swimming between 6 pm and 6 am, no standing on dunes, no digging holes deeper than 18 inches, no open fires without a permit, etc. Be sure to read all the signs when you arrive at the beach.

SWIMMING 6AM-6PM ONLY

What did the sea say to the sand?

Nothing. It just waved.

ARE YOU SUN SAVVY?

Everyone loves coming home with souvenirs from the beach, unless the souvenir is a nasty sunburn. Who wants to look as red as a lobster or peel like a banana? Sunburn damages your skin and can lead to health problems as you get older. Protect it! It's the only skin you have.

◆ Use a waterproof sunscreen and apply it before heading to the beach. Don't forget hands, ears, feet, shoulders, and behind the neck. An SPF lip balm is a must. Cracked lips are gross!

◆ Reapply sunscreen often, at least every 2–3 hours and always after swimming.

◆ The sun is hottest between 10 am and 4 pm, so if you get too hot or tired during this time, take a short break and settle down in the shade with a magazine, eat lunch, or play a game.

◆ Sunglasses are like sunscreen for your eyes. Get a pair that has UV protection.

◆ Drink plenty of water to keep cool and hydrated.

◆ Wear a hat! Who wants a dry, itchy scalp?

BLOCK THOSE ULTRAVIOLET RAYS!

The SPF (Sun Protection Factor) number on your bottle of sunscreen is important. It measures how long you can stay in the sun without being burned by ultraviolet rays. The higher the SPF number, the more protection the sunscreen will provide, and the longer you can stay in the sun without being burned. Ask an adult what SPF number is best for you, and remember to reapply sunscreen every 2 hours for the best results.

How much does it cost for a pirate to have his ears pierced?

A buck-an-ear

Do sunscreens really work? You decide! Get a piece of dark blue or red construction paper and cut it out in the shape of a bubble person. Coat the arms, legs, and head of the paper cut-out with different SPF sunscreens. Be sure to mark which sunscreen you used on each body part. Place the bubble person in direct sunlight for several hours. What happened to the exposed part of the body? Compare the different body parts protected by varying SPF sunscreens. Which one worked best?

BE SAFE, STAY SAFE!

A trip to the beach wouldn't be complete without a dip in the ocean. Before you dive in, make sure you know these safety tips.

1. *Never* swim alone and *always* swim near a lifeguard.

2. Swim between flags that mark safe zones.

3. Don't chew gum or eat while you're in the ocean.

4. Don't dunk or jump on other swimmers.

5. Don't use inflatable toys or rafts in deep water because they could deflate or tip over. Use a life jacket instead.

6. If you're caught in a rip tide or strong current, swim sideways until free. Don't swim against the current's pull.

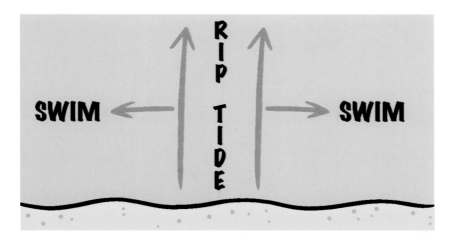

7. Always jump feet first into unknown waters to avoid hurting your head or neck.

8. If you're in trouble, call or wave for help. Now is NOT the time to be shy.

9. If a lifeguard is waving or blowing a whistle in your direction, he's trying to get your attention. Pay attention . . . he isn't just being friendly!

10. Never turn your back to the ocean. You could be swept away by a wave that comes without warning.

11. If you like to swim long distances, swim parallel to the shore, not away from the shore into deep water.

12. Pay attention to weather conditions and forecasts. Stop swimming at the first sign of bad weather.

Which day of the week is the least favorite for a fish?

FRYday

Seaside Fun

Y ou've got the whole day to play at the beach. With these activities, you and your friends can enjoy hours of fun.

BOTTLE UP YOUR THOUGHTS

When you stand in front of the ocean, do you wonder who's playing on the beach on the other side? Why not send a message in a bottle and find out?

What you need:

- Clear plastic bottle with a twist-on top
- Dry sand
- Paper and pen
- Electrical or duct tape

What you do:

1. Write a note on a piece of paper. It should include the city and country you're from, the date, and a friendly "hello" message. If you really want a reply, include a self-addressed stamped envelope.

2. Fill the bottle with 1 inch of dry sand so it'll float.

3. Roll up your note and push it into the bottle.

4. Twist the lid on tight and then wrap tape around the lid to seal it.

5. Toss it into the ocean. If possible, drop it off of a boat or a fishing pier so the waves don't bring it right back to the shore.

6. Wait for a reply and be patient! One family in Florida got their bottle back nineteen years after tossing it into the sea!

SEASIDE TOSS

What you need:

- Firm, slightly wet sand so you can draw on it with a stick or the heel of your foot
- Shell or stick

Make this game even more fun by marking each section with an action!

Hop on one foot

Run down to the surf and back

Do a hula dance

Shout, "Beach Party!" three times

Run around the board backwards

What you do:

1. Draw a large square in the sand using a stick or the heel of your foot. Divide the square into smaller, irregular-shaped sections. Inside each section, use a shell, stick, or other object to write +5, -3, +10, +1, -5, Double, Triple, Lose Turn, and others.

2. Draw a line about ten paces from the square and mark the spot to stand behind. From there, the first player must toss a shell or pebble onto the game board.

3. If the player misses the board, his or her turn is over. If he or she hits a target, he or she gets whatever is in that section. Aim carefully or you could start off with a negative number!

4. Keep playing until everyone has ten turns. Keep track of the scores; the person with the most points wins.

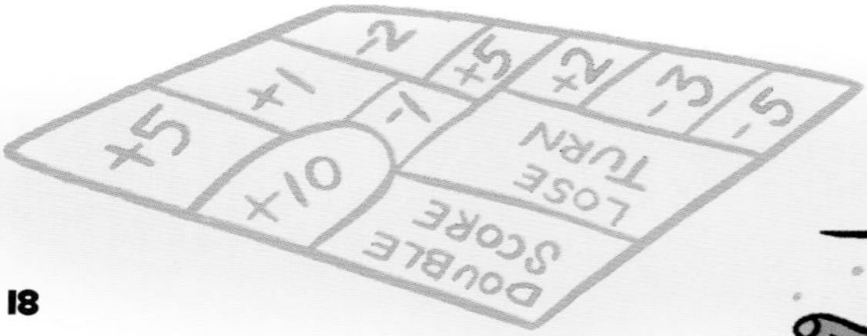

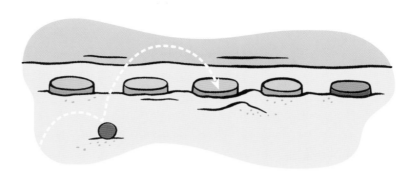

BUCKET BLINKO

What you need:
- ◆ Five sand buckets
- ◆ Tennis ball

What you do:
1. Play this game near the water's edge where the sand is firm enough for a ball to bounce.

2. Bury the five buckets in a row, about a foot apart so the rims are just a few inches above the sand's surface.

3. Try to get the ball into the first bucket by throwing and making it bounce *once* before landing in the bucket. If you miss, your turn is over. If you make it, you get another turn.

4. On the next turn, try to bounce the ball into the second bucket.

5. Keep going until a player gets Blinko, which is bouncing the ball into each bucket in order.

WALK THE PLANK

What you need:

- ◆ At least 3 people, but more is better
- ◆ 2 water guns
- ◆ 2 beach towels that are the same size
- ◆ 12 shells, rocks, or sticks

What you do:

1. Set up the beach towels side by side. Spread 6 shells, rocks, or sticks across the length of each towel, evenly spaced.

2. Two players hold the water guns and stand at one end of each towel. They take turns trying to hit the other players (who are running around like moving targets) with one squirt of water.

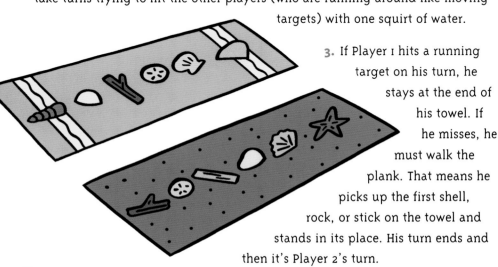

3. If Player 1 hits a running target on his turn, he stays at the end of his towel. If he misses, he must walk the plank. That means he picks up the first shell, rock, or stick on the towel and stands in its place. His turn ends and then it's Player 2's turn.

4. Each time Player 1 or 2 misses a target, he or she must walk the plank by moving forward to the next marker on the towel. Once a player runs out of markers, he or she has to jump off of his or her plank and the other player still standing wins!

5. Once there is a winner, have Player 1 and Player 2 switch places with two of the moving targets and then play again so everyone has a chance to do both!

What gets wetter as you get drier?

A beach towel

SHARKS AND STINGRAYS

This game works well in waist-deep water with a group of kids that can be broken up into two groups. The groups could be boys and girls, short hair and long hair, or T-shirts and no T-shirts.

What you do:

1. Divide the kids evenly, and name one group Sharks and the other Stingrays. Both groups face each other about 15 feet apart. An adult player calls out one of the names, for example, STINGRAYS!

2. The Stingray group swims toward the Shark group and tries to tag members of the opposite group. Anyone tagged must go and sit on the beach.

3. Here's the fun part! Every 15 to 25 seconds, the adult calls out the name of the other group, in this case, SHARKS! Suddenly, the hunters now become the hunted and the Sharks must now chase and tag the Stingrays. One team wins when all the players from the other team are sitting on the beach.

HIGH TIDE LOW TIDE

Just like the tides come in and go out, you'll be running in and out of the water for this game!

What you need:
- ◆ 2 beach balls
- ◆ 2 or more players

What you do:

1. First, pick a home base about 50 feet from the ocean. Make sure there are 2 beach balls there. The players start at home base, ready to race against each other.

2. Next, players should do a crab walk down to the ocean. Once there, players get up and race into the ocean, jumping or diving under the first wave. Then, they must run out of the water and get back to home base.

3. Once back at home base, they have to grab a beach ball, place it between their knees, and run down to the water. After dropping the ball in the water, they run out into the water and jump over or dive under the next wave again. The winner is the first one to make it back to home base.

4. If more than two kids play, split into two teams and have each player complete the whole process.

5. The team that finishes everything first wins.

Other Fun Beach Games

Horseshoes
Volleyball
Paddleball
Dodgeball
Frisbee
Frisbee Baseball
Kite-flying
Football
Tag

Hangman
Long Jump Contest
Hopscotch
Four Corners
Tic-Tac-Toe
Wiffle Ball
Kickball

Tide Pools

You can get a peek at life under the sea by looking into a tide pool. Tide pools are formed when the tide goes out and leaves pockets of water behind. They are usually found in rocky areas on the edge of the ocean that are filled with seawater. Plants and creatures live there. Look closely and you may find starfish, anemones, urchins, crabs, seaweed, and countless other living things.

Stay still for a while and just watch. These creatures are masters of disguise. That rock just may turn out to be a crab! Remember, don't disturb their habitat. Look, but don't touch!

SEASIDE AQUARIUM

If you can't find a tide pool, make a seaside aquarium so you can study ocean life.

What you need:

◆ A large clear container
◆ Sand

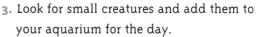

What you do:

1. Fill the bottom of the container with sand.

2. Add seawater, seaweed, plants, small rocks, pebbles, driftwood, shells . . . whatever you find in the ocean.

3. Look for small creatures and add them to your aquarium for the day.

4. When you leave the beach, return everything to the place you found it and then dump the aquarium right back into the ocean.

TIP: *Forget adding jellyfish. They sting!*

WHY DOES THE OCEAN HAVE SALT IN IT?

Salt is a mineral that comes from the earth. It's stored in deposits in the land and in rocks and sediments below the ocean floor. When rivers run through mountains, farmlands, and valleys, they accumulate all kinds of minerals from the rocks and soil and then deposit them when they flow into the ocean. Salt dissolves easily in water. Since it can't evaporate with water into the atmosphere, the level of salt in the ocean has been slowly building over the years, causing the remaining water to become saltier and saltier as time passes. Ocean water evaporates and freezes into polar ice. Either way, the salt it brought with it is left behind.

TIP: *Don't bring home ocean life thinking you can plunk them into a tank of water and add table salt. The animals and plants will die. There are other minerals in the sea that you can't duplicate at home.*

"SEA" FOR YOURSELF!

This experiment will let you observe the evaporation process. Be sure to set this up outside in direct sunlight.

What you need:

◆ 1 cup ocean water
◆ Cookie sheet
◆ Black construction paper

What you do:

1. Cover the bottom of the cookie sheet with black construction paper.

2. Pour the water over the paper.

3. Set the tray in a sunny spot where it won't be disturbed.

4. Over the next few days, the water will evaporate and leave a thin layer of salt behind.

TIP: *Since the amount of salt varies greatly from ocean to ocean, redo the experiment on your next vacation. If the ocean is near a body of freshwater, you won't have as much salt in the water sample.*

SAND, SAND, EVERYWHERE!

No matter what beach you go to, you can't escape SAND! It will find its way down your bathing suit, into your ears, onto your ice cream sandwich, and into your bag. But a day at the beach is worth it, isn't it?

Just what is sand and why is there so much of it? When the ocean knocks around rocks, shells, and minerals, tiny bits flake off and become sand one grain at a time. Depending on the shells and rocks in your area, the sand could be white, green, black (like lava rocks in Hawaii), pink (like coral in Bermuda), tan, and just about any range in between. It could be very fine, coarse, or so sharp and jagged that you need to wear your flip-flops when walking on it.

START A SAND COLLECTION

What you need:

- Notebook and pen
- Ziplock bag or
  film canister
- Marker
- Sand sample
- Tape

What you do:

1. Every time you visit a beach,
fill up a baggie or a small film canister
with some sand. Label it with the date and the location of the beach.

2. Record the information in a notebook.

3. Sprinkle a few grains of sand in the notebook and put clear tape over it so
you have a quick view of the sand and can compare samples.

TIP: *When your friends or family members travel to a beach, ask them to
bring you back a baggie of the sand. Soon, you'll have samples from all over
the world!*

What is black and white with red all over?

A sunburned zebra.

BEACHCOMBING

Walk along the water's edge at low tide and look for sea treasures that the waves pushed ashore. Besides shells, seaweed, and sea glass, maybe you'll get lucky and find a fossilized shark's tooth, a conch, or an egg case from a whelk.

Maybe you'll see a coconut wash ashore. Where did it come from? You know that it came from a palm tree on the beach, but you just won't know which beach or how far it traveled. The driftwood that washed up may be from an old shipwreck. Can you spot crab shells or claws? It's often possible to find an entire crab. Keep away from jellyfish!

Beachcombing is the most common way to collect shells. Did you know that all seashells were once homes to some form of sea life? The hard shell offered the soft-bodied creature protection.

When you collect shells, make sure you take only the empty ones. If you pick one up and discover something living inside, gently put it back where you found it. Some people dive for shells, buy them in stores, or trade them with friends. Before you collect shells, make sure it's permitted. Several beaches have laws against collecting shells because tourists have taken too many. Some people believe that you should take a picture of a beautiful shell with your camera and leave the shell where it is since its part of a fragile ecosystem. Who knows? A hermit crab might be planning to move into it!

TIP: *You must take out any remains of previous inhabitants of the shell to prevent odor. Be sure to gently wash your shells before bringing them inside your house.*

If you decide to collect shells, just take one of each kind that you see and leave the others for another beachcomber. You can check out a book on shells from the library and learn the names of the ones you found.

Some shells have interesting names. See if you can guess why they earned their name. If you find a shell and don't know what its true name is, make up your own!

 Mussel

Cockleshell

Sea Urchin

Pen

 **Razor Clam**

 Periwinkle

 Shark's Eye

Sand Dollar

 Scallop

Branded Tulip

Fighting Conch

Turkey Wing

Oyster

Cat's Paw

 Whelk

Slipper

Worm Shell

Sand Sculptures

Making sand castles and sand sculptures is one of the best ways to play at the beach. Besides a castle, try some of these sand sculpture ideas:

◆ *A mermaid with seaweed for her hair.*

◆ *An octopus with eight wiggly tentacles.*

◆ *Your house with a stick family in the doorway.*

◆ *A plane, train, or car that you can sit in.*

◆ *A sea monster with shell teeth and eyes.*

Crafts to Tide You Over

C rafts with a beach theme are a great inexpensive way to remember the good times you had at the shore.

VACATION JAR

Did you collect a little of this and a little of that? Do you have some mementos that can't fit into a scrapbook? Make a Vacation Jar!

What you need:

- Glass jar with lid
- Sand
- Beach treasures you've collected, such as dried starfish, shells, sea glass, dried seaweed, your beach badge, pebbles, postcard, small photo, a piece of saltwater taffy, and any other objects that remind you the beach.

What you do:

1. Fill one-third or so of the jar with sand.

2. Add your treasures, arranging them so everything can be seen.

3. Screw the lid on tightly and display.

TIP: *You can decorate the lid of your Vacation Jar too. Some decoration ideas: tie a raffia bow around the neck of the bottle; paint the lid a color that complements the glass or glue shells onto it.*

Sea Glass

What's the perfect way to show off all of the sea glass you found? In a glass jar, of course! Fill a decorated jar with the sea glass. Then, place the jar on a windowsill so the sun can shine through the jar. Your glass will sparkle just as it did in the sand.

PICTURE-PERFECT

You caught a huge fish while fishing on a pier? Built the most dazzling sand castle? Prove it . . . with photos! Here are three picture-perfect projects that will make you smile and say, "Cheese."

Catch-My-Drift Frame

What you need:

- Plain wooden picture frame
- Bits of driftwood, shells, and sea glass
- Paint or markers
- Glue

What you do:

1. Paint or color the picture frame and let dry.

2. Glue items on the sides and top of frame. Leave the bottom empty.

3. In the empty space, write with the paint or marker the name of the beach and the date you were there.

4. Insert your beach picture and display.

Sand-Sational Picture Frames

These picture frames make great gifts for friends and family.

What you need:

- ◆ Clear, empty CD case
- ◆ Sand
- ◆ Glue
- ◆ Small shells or beach items (seaweed, driftwood, sea glass, etc.)
- ◆ Photo
- ◆ Tape

What you do:

1. Open the see-through CD case and tape the picture to the right-hand side in the middle. You can put the tape on the back of the picture so it can't be seen. Close the CD case.

2. Spread glue on top of the CD case around the picture.

3. Cover the glue with sand and then shake off excess.

4. Glue small shells or beach items onto the sand.

5. Wait until it's completely dry before you move it or give it to a friend.

What washes up on very small beaches?

Microwaves

Frozen-in-Time Frames

You can search for discarded Popsicle sticks or, even better, slurp down a dozen on your own. Start licking!

What you need:

- 10 Popsicle sticks
- Acrylic paints
- Brushes
- Cardboard
- Glue
- Magnet
- Photo

What you do:

1. Collect and rinse off the Popsicle sticks.

2. Glue them onto a piece of cardboard. (The cardboard should be about $1/2$ inch shorter than the sticks.)

3. Paint the sticks and let them dry completely.

4. Glue your picture onto the sticks.

5. Use a marker to draw swirls or shapes on the rest of the sticks, and add a title that goes with your picture.

LOOK LIKE A BEACH BUM

Whether you're a surfer, a sunbather, or a swimmer, you'll look cool with these accessories!

No-Sink Keychain

Need to keep your house key with you at all times? You can blink and it won't sink! Make this keychain, and while you're crabbing, fishing, or surfing, you won't have to worry about losing your key because it will float.

What you need:
◆ Cork
◆ Paint
◆ Yarn
◆ Screwdriver

What to do:
1. Paint the cork a bright color so it's easy to spot in case it ends up in the water.

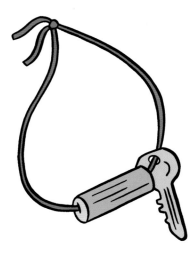

2. With a thin screwdriver, gently tunnel your way through the cork. Ask an adult for help with this part.

3. Thread yarn through the cork.

4. Place key on yarn and tie the ends. It floats!

Trendy Towels

Soak up some fun with this towel! Why bring an ordinary towel to the beach when you can bring an extraordinary one? It makes a great souvenir, too.

What you need:
- ◆ Large solid-colored towel
- ◆ Nontoxic fabric paints
- ◆ Paint brushes

What you do:

1. Have your beach buddies dip their hand or foot into fabric paint.

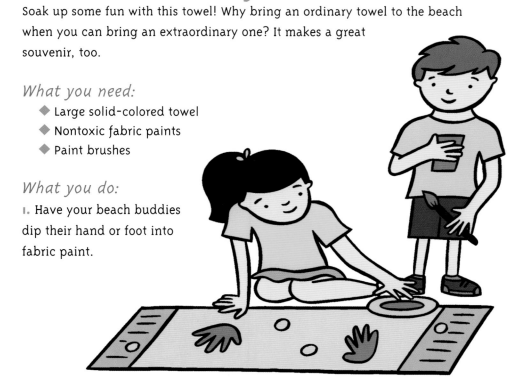

2. Have them press their hand or foot down on the towel and then let the paint dry according to directions.

3. Have your friends/family write names beneath their print. You can add prints year after year.

4. Let the paint dry for at least 24 hours before using.

Brag Bag

Towel, sunscreen, comb, magazine, water bottle . . . where do you stash all this stuff? In a BRAG BAG! A mesh bag is the best choice for the beach so the sand can sift through the openings. But if you're a surfer dude or dudette, a cute mesh bag won't cut it. Convert your backpack into a Brag Bag.

What you need:
◆ Backpack
◆ Fabric paint
◆ Paint brushes
◆ Craft foam
◆ Plastic hook

What you do:

1. Paint a cool beach phrase on the backpack.

2. Paint a shark, dolphin, or other ocean creature on the front pocket.

3. Decorate the backpack with paints, using swirls, squiggles, or whatever!

4. Let the paint dry completely.

5. Cut out a 3-inch piece of foam in the shape of a surfboard. Decorate it with other pieces of craft foam so it looks like your favorite surfboard.

6. Make a small hole near the top of the surfboard and insert your hook. It makes a great zipper pull!

Some popular beach phrases:

Catch a Wave	*I Love the Beach*
Hang Ten	*Beach Bum*
Life's a Beach	*Beach Babe*
Surf's Up	*Toes on the Nose*
Get Stoked	*Catchin' Rays*

Flops To Make You Flip

Flip-flops are the best kind of footwear at the beach. They're easy to slip on and off, and the sand just slides right out! These are a lot of fun to make and they're really stylish. Plan on creating a few pairs to give away!

What you need:

◆ Pair of flip-flops
◆ ½ yard of ribbon or fabric
◆ Scissors

What you do:

1. Cut strips of fabric or ribbon into 2- to 4-inch lengths (depending on size of your foot) and various widths.

2. Tie the fabric onto the top of the flip-flop (starting in the middle and working out), making just one knot. Repeat until the strap is full.

TIP: *Mix and match patterns and textures. How about black ribbon mixed in with pink polka-dotted fabric? Feeling patriotic? Try red, white, and blue! Solid yellow ribbon paired with yellow-striped ribbon? You could even thread the ends with big beads and tie a knot.*

Beach Bash!

A beach-themed party is the perfect way to kick off or end the summer season. It's also a blast to have an indoor party during the cold winter months. Everything you need to know about organizing and planning the party is right here. So, fill up your neighbor's wading pools with sand, break out the beach towels and chairs, plunk little paper umbrellas into Berry-Licious Blender Slurps (see page 57), and get ready for a party that's so cool, it's Hot! Hot! Hot!

INVITATIONS

Invitations set the mood for a party. You could just call your friends to invite them (boring!), or you could get creative and send them one of these festive invitations.

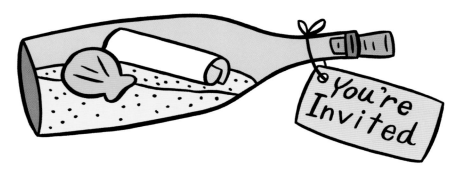

Invitation in a Bottle

What you need:

◆ Paper and pens
◆ Empty plastic water bottles, one for each invitation
◆ Sand, tiny shells, sea glass, and other small items found on the beach

What you do:

1. Write the party information down on the paper: who, what, where, why, when.

2. Roll up the paper and put it inside the bottle.

3. Fill the bottle with a handful of sand, small shells, and other beach items.

4. Deliver to your friends.

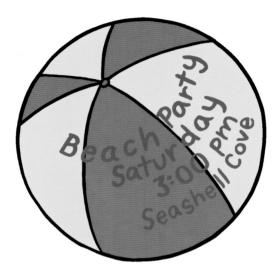

Beach Ball Invitation

What you need:

◆ Blow-up beach balls, one for
   each invitation
◆ Permanent marker

What you do:

1. While the ball is deflated, write the
party info on the ball.

2. Blow up the ball and deliver it to your
friends. They'll have all your party
details and something fun to play with!

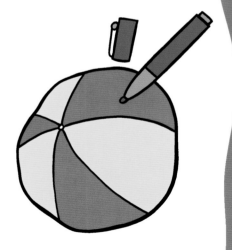

Sunglasses Invitation

These shades make the grade!

What you need:

- ◆ Inexpensive sunglasses or play sunglasses, one for each invitation
- ◆ Paper
- ◆ Marker
- ◆ Curling ribbon

What you do:

1. Trace the lenses of the sunglasses onto paper and then cut them out.

2. Write party info on the paper lenses and then glue onto the real lenses.

3. Add curling ribbon in bright colors at the center.

4. Deliver or mail to your friends.

TIP: *Be sure to include an RSVP date. After all, you need to know how much food to make.*

TWO, FOUR, SIX, EIGHT! GET READY TO DECORATE!

Any craft or party store should have decorations for your bash. Depending on your budget, you can buy paper centerpieces like pineapples or coconuts, pirate eye patches, candy treasure, grass table skirts, leis, large paper flowers, tropical-themed paper plates, palm trees, etc. No budget? No problem! Gather up kiddie pools, beach chairs, towels, inflatable boats or tubs, beach balls, and a surfboard, and you're good to go!

TIP: *Fill the inflatable boat or tub with ice and store your drinks in it. Guests can serve themselves.*

TIP: *Use a clean sand mold in the shape of a shell or fish to freeze ice (add food coloring). Use it in a punch bowl to add decoration to a cooler full of drinks, etc.*

Why couldn't the pirate play cards?
He was sitting on the deck.

Setting a "beachy" mood for your party is easy and doesn't have to cost a dime. Look around your house for items that'll help make the party look festive. Grab your Christmas twinkle lights and string them around your doors, deck, and bushes or shrubs. Tiki torches and Chinese lanterns will brighten up the place. Don't be shy: ask your travel agent for leftover posters that feature exotic beach locations and hang them around. Your local grocer can save the discarded tops of pineapples for you if you ask. Group a bunch of them together for centerpieces and spread some pretty shells around the base to create an instant tropical feeling. Move

the TV and DVD player outside and have a beach movie on in the background. Let your (or a friend's) pet goldfish take center stage as the centerpiece on top of the TV or a table. And, of course, don't forget colorful beach balls: hang them around the deck, from doorways and ceilings (use double-sided tape), and toss some on the ground. Your guests are sure to have a ball!

TIP: *The mood needs to be set the second your friends arrive at your house. If the party's out back, have several sets of flip-flops leading the way (like a person walking) around back with signs marking the way: Beach Bash This Way, Beach Hours 7–10 pm, No Fishing From Pier, Surf's Up, High Tide, etc. (Use poster board to make the signs, attach to sticks, and push them into the ground or a sand-filled bucket.) Along the "path," set up a "beach scene" with lots of props: beach chair, towel, umbrella, sunglasses, Frisbees, bucket and shovel, a deck of cards, and suntan lotion.*

The key ingredient to a great beach party is FOOD! Ask mom or dad to fire up the grill and make burgers and hot dogs for the main course while you concentrate on snacks and dessert.

 If hamburgers and hot dogs aren't tropical enough, get help to make a meal that your friends will love or try some of these tasty recipes!

Coconut Chicken Strips

What you need:

- 1 cup shredded coconut
- ½ cup flour
- ½ teaspoon salt
- ½ teaspoon black pepper
- ¼ teaspoon garlic powder
- 1 pound boneless chicken breasts, cut into 1-inch strips
- 2 eggs, beaten
- ⅓ cup margarine or butter, melted

What you do:

1. Preheat oven to 400 degrees.

2. Mix coconut, flour, salt, pepper, and garlic powder in a bowl.

3. Dip chicken strips into eggs and then coat with coconut mixture.

4. Place strips in a baking dish and drizzle butter on top.

5. Bake for 15 minutes; turn. Bake another 10 minutes.

SERVES 6

Bucket-and-Shovel Cake

Here's a cake that's *shore* to be scooped up! Dig in!

What you need:

- ◆ 1 baked cake (8- or 9-inch round layers)
- ◆ 1 new bucket and shovel
- ◆ 2 (3-ounce) packages instant vanilla pudding (prepared)
- ◆ 2 cups crushed graham crackers
- ◆ Fish or shell candies

What you do:

1. Cut the cake into 1-inch pieces.

2. Alternate layers (in bucket) of cake pieces with vanilla pudding, ending with a layer of pudding.

3. Sprinkle on crushed crackers (it looks like sand) and garnish with the candy and the shovel.

SERVES 10

**Which day is the best day
to go to the beach?**

SUNday.

Fruity Kabobs

What you need:

- ◆ 1 cup each of different fruit, such as pineapple chunks, melons, strawberries, grapes, etc.
- ◆ 30 squares of brownies, about 1 inch
- ◆ Long wooden skewers

What you do:

1. Cut up pineapples, melons, and strawberries into chunks. No need to cut the grapes!

2. Carefully thread fruit pieces and brownie squares onto the skewers, about 5 to 6 items per kabob.

3. Serve kabobs to your guests on new Frisbees.

SERVES 8

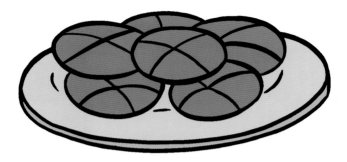

Beach Ball Cookies

What you need:

- ◆ 2 dozen store-bought sugar cookies
- ◆ 2 (8-ounce) cans white frosting
- ◆ Food coloring, 2 to 4 colors
- ◆ Bowls
- ◆ Spoons
- ◆ Knives, one for each color

What you do:

1. Separate white frosting equally into bowls. Add a few drops of food coloring into each bowl so you have different-colored frostings.

2. Start in the center and work down. Use the frosting to "paint" four triangles on the cookie.

MAKES 2 DOZEN

TIP: *Instead of making these before-hand, have everyone make their own at the party.*

Berry-Licious Blender Slurps

It's fun to offer blender drinks at a beach bash if an adult helps make them.

What you need:

- ◆ 1 container lemonade
- ◆ 1 cup water
- ◆ 6 ice cubes
- ◆ 2 cups fresh or frozen straw-berries (or other fruit)

What you do:

1. Pour 3 cups of lemonade into the blender.

2. Add remaining ingredients and cover.

3. Blend on high speed for 15 seconds.

4. Pour into a plastic cup and serve with a little paper umbrella!

What does a crab use to call someone?

A SHELLular phone.

Your food table should look spectacular. Make sure you have at least one long table for your spread. If you need more space, ask mom or dad for a card table. Find some sturdy boxes or piles of books and arrange them on the table at different heights. Cover the table (books and boxes, too!) with two blue table-cloths. Have any fishing net? Drape over the table and put shells and sea stars around. Serve all of your salads, chips, and dip in clean buckets and shovels.

TIP: *Goldfish crackers come in all sorts of colors. Besides putting bowls of them around to munch on, sprinkle some ON the table for a nice touch.*

SPLISH, SPLASH! HAVE FUN AT THE BASH

Music is a must! Grab the nearest Beach Boys CD and pop it in. There are lots of activities you can do while you're jamming to some beach tunes.

Limbo Limbo

Grab a broomstick or long stick, pump up the music, and let the fun begin. Have two people hold the ends of the stick at shoulder level while everyone else gets in a line. Each person goes under the stick while leaning backward. In order to advance to the next round, no body part (except feet!) can touch the stick or ground. It's easy at first but each round gets harder as you lower the stick a few inches at a time. The winner is the last one who makes it under the stick without falling or touching it. So, how low can you and your friends go?

Hula Hoop Contest

Have plenty of hula hoops around because once your friends see others doing it, they'll want to join in. Start with a hoop around your waist and see who can keep it spinning the longest. How about putting a hoop on each arm and spinning both at once? Try spinning one around your waist and one on your arm at the same time. Easier said than done! Feeling adventurous? How about both arms and one leg at the same time! The winner gets to take a hula hoop home.

Why can't you starve on a beach?
Because of all the sand which is there.

Coconut Bowling

This is a game that takes seconds to set up but provides hours of fun. Grab a few coconuts and rinse out 10 soda cans. Set up the cans in a triangle (1 can in front, 2 behind it, then 3 cans followed by 4 in the back row.) Place a stick about fifteen feet from the cans. Each player must stand behind the stick and roll a coconut toward the cans to knock them down. Each player gets two tries per turn. After your turn, record the number of cans knocked down as your score and reset the cans for the next person. The first person to knock down a total of 50 cans wins.

Tip: *Don't forget to set up the Slip 'n' Slide, a volleyball net, and a sprinkler, or have a karaoke contest (with Beach Boys songs of course!).*

EDIBLE SAND ART

This is a fun party favor that your friends can make before leaving.

What you need:

- small clear containers, such as tubes or baby food jars
- Pixie Stix
- Toothpicks (optional)

What you do:

1. Pour several of the same color of Pixie Stix into the bottom of your tube or jar to create a layer of color.

2. Next pour in several of a second Pixie Stix color to create a second layer. If you want, make designs using a toothpick around the sides and slightly mix the colors.

3. Finish by layering more colors and adding designs with the toothpick if desired. Now it's ready to eat!

Beach Party 2006

ALOHA!

There's one more thing to do before you say **aloha** (the Hawaiian word for both hello and good-bye) to your guests. Have an adult take a picture of you and all your guests. Now that's a fabulous ending to a picture-perfect party!

Collect 'em All!

Available at bookstores or directly
from GIBBS SMITH, PUBLISHER
1.800.748.5439
www.gibbs-smith.com

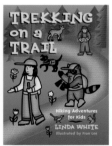